Introduce
little monkey;
poseful adventures. Matthew will win your heart y—
will fall in love with him…just like I did!

Mary Beth Egeling
Author of *Love-abouts* and *Messages from My Hands*

Matthew the monkey is a character who is sure to appeal to young children and parents alike. The situations in which Matthew finds himself reflect real life concerns a young child may encounter. Mrs. Swart writes with a style that demonstrates a true sensitivity to these concerns, and through compassion and humor she assures us that each story will reach a genuine and satisfying conclusion. In addition, the stories offer parents the opportunity to discuss openly and honestly with children the fears and challenges the child may face. These stories are very enjoyable, and children are sure to request hearing them over and over again!

William Schoff
Author of *Something Strange*
and *I'm Not Feeling Like Myself Today*

The Adventures of
Matthew
THE Monkey

The best adventure
is a shared adventure

Sharon
Swair
8-2012

The Adventures of Matthew THE Monkey

BY
SHARON SWART

tate publishing
CHILDREN'S DIVISION

Published by Tate Publishing & Enterprises, LLC
127 E. Trade Center Terrace | Mustang, Oklahoma 73064 USA
1.888.361.9473 | www.tatepublishing.com

Tate Publishing is committed to excellence in the publishing industry. The company reflects the philosophy established by the founders, based on Psalm 68:11,
"The Lord gave the word and great was the company of those who published it."

Published in the United States of America

ISBN: 978-1-62024-411-1
1. Juvenile Fiction, Social Issues, Values & Virtues
2. Juvenile Fiction, Social Issues, New Experience
12.07.17

DEDICATION

To Lloyd, Justin, Keith, Megan, and Brian,
who are always there to share in my life's adventures.

TABLE OF CONTENTS

MATTHEW
AND OPENING DAY

Matthew the monkey is five years old. He lives in a tree house with his mom and dad, his older brother Michael, and younger sister Madeline. Matthew and his family live in a jungle community called Mango Grove. The citizens of the grove all get along nicely. For Matthew, Mango Grove is a perfect place to grow up and have many adventures.

It was Thursday, and Matthew was starting to get excited about this Saturday's opening day baseball game. Opening day meant the official start to summer. Ever since Matthew was two years old, he and his dad went to the game together. It was a tradition.

Matthew had already picked out the clothes he was going to wear to the game. He had a jersey with the team logo on it and a pair of blue sweatpants. He set aside his baseball mitt too. Neither he nor Dad had ever caught a fly ball, but they always wanted to be prepared.

That night at dinner, Matthew talked non-stop about where they were going to sit and what kind of snacks they were going to eat and how maybe they might even catch a fly ball this year.

After dinner, Matthew and his brother Michael went outside to play catch. Mom and Dad stayed at the kitchen table.

"How am I going to break the news to him that I cannot go to the game this Saturday? It will break his heart," said Dad.

"I cannot believe that they scheduled the seminar for work this weekend," added Mom.

"I tried to get out of it, but I can't. Well, I can't put this off any longer. I need to tell him."

Dad went out to the backyard. He told Michael that he needed to speak with Matthew alone. "Matthew, come have a seat next to me," said Dad as he patted the step next to him. Matthew sat down next to dad. "What's going on, Dad? You seem so sad," asked Matthew.

"Well, I am a little sad. I have something to tell you, and it is difficult for me because I know that it will make you sad too."

Matthew was getting a little nervous. "What is it, Dad?"

"On Saturday, I have to attend a seminar at work. I have tried to get out of it, but I can't. I have to attend the seminar. I'm sorry."

Matthew thought for a minute and then realized that Saturday was the opening day game and that dad was telling him that he could not go to the game with him. "That's not fair!" cried Matthew as he got up and ran into the house, slamming the kitchen door. He ran through the kitchen and right up to his room.

"I see that it did not go well," said Mom as Dad came in and sat down in his recliner.

"No." He sighed. "Not well at all."

"I'll speak to him later. He just needs time to process the news."

Later that night, as Matthew got ready for bed, Mom came in to read him a story before lights out.

"I don't feel like a story tonight, Mom," said Matthew.

"Then let's just talk. You know that your dad loves you and would never do anything to intentionally make you sad. He feels as badly as you do about not being able to go with you to the game. I know I'm not your dad, but I would love to go with you to the opening day game. I like baseball too."

"I don't know," said Matthew.

"Well, think about it, and let me know tomorrow," said Mom as she kissed him goodnight.

The next morning at breakfast, Matthew told his mom that he would still like to go to the game. He said it would not be the same without Dad, but he thanked his mom for pinch-hitting.

Finally, opening day had arrived. Matthew put on his jersey and sweatpants and had his mitt with him as he came down for breakfast. On the table was a mitt he had never seen before.

"Hey, whose mitt is this?" asked Matthew.

"It's mine," said Mom.

"What! I didn't know that you knew how to play baseball."

"I sure do, and I was pretty good at it too. Now let's go have some fun."

Matthew and Mom said good-bye to Michael and Madeline. Michael was getting old enough to babysit. He loved being with Madeline, and he was earning a little money too.

There was a large crowd for opening day, and Matthew and Mom found great seats right in line with first base.

"Sometimes foul balls get hit this way, so watch out, Mom," said Matthew.

"I will. Thanks for the warning."

The game started. Matthew and Mom ate something from every vendor that passed by. They had peanuts, popcorn, cotton candy, nachos, and hot dogs. They cheered for their team and laughed at the silly mascot.

With mustard on his cheek and a mouthful of hot dog, Matthew said, "Thanks for being with me, Mom. I'm having such a great time."

"You are very welcome. I'm having fun too," said Mom, and she smiled back at Matthew.

At the seventh inning stretch, they sang "Take Me out to the Ball Game," and Matthew's mom got picked to throw the beanbags in the barrel.

Matthew watched from the sideline as Mom stepped out onto the field.

"Come on, Mom, you can do it!" shouted Matthew.

Mom took aim, Matthew held his breath, and she tossed the beanbag right into the barrel. The crowd cheered, and Matthew ran out onto the field to give his mom a hug. She won free tickets for their family for the next home game.

Back in their seats, they watched the rest of the game. At the last inning, their team was ahead by only one run. If their team could hold them this inning, they would win. There were two outs, and one of the other team's best hitters was up to bat. The first pitch flew by.

"Strike one!" yelled the umpire.

The crowd cheered. The second pitch was a little slower, and the batter connected, but it was going foul. It was headed right toward Matthew and his mom. Everyone around them stood up, trying to catch the ball. Matthew lost sight of it; he then sat down, not sure where the ball had ended up.

"Looking for this?" asked Mom as she handed Matthew the ball.

"What? You caught the ball!" yelled Matthew.

"Yes, I guess I still have it," said Mom, smiling. What an amazing day. Their team had won. Matthew's mom won tickets to the next home game, and she even caught a fly ball.

That night as she tucked Matthew in to bed, he thanked her again for going with him.

"I can't wait for tomorrow to tell Dad all about the game," said Matthew.

※　※　※

The next day when Dad got home, Matthew talked non-stop, reliving every moment. He told him about how he and Mom ate everything the vendors sold, how they sang and cheered, how Mom won the tickets for the next home game, and how she amazingly caught a foul ball.

"I'm really looking forward to the next game," said Dad. "I'll have to find my mitt."

"I can't wait either, Dad," said Matthew. "But let's let only Mom bring her mitt. Her record of catching foul balls is much better than yours."

MATTHEW
CLIMBS UP HIGH

It was Monday and the first day of summer camp for Matthew and Michael. The boys were finishing up their breakfast of mango oatmeal.

"I'm going to climb to the top of the jungle gym this year!" said Matthew.

"Oh, be careful, sweetie," answered Mom. "It's very high. I'm not sure that you are ready to climb all the way up to the top yet."

"I was eight years old before I could climb to the top," said Michael. "Maybe you should wait until next summer."

"No," said Matthew, "I'm climbing to the top this summer."

"Boys, let's get going," said Dad. "We have to pick up Grant and Christopher, and you don't want to be late on your first day at camp." Grant is a young lion, and he is Michael's best friend. Christopher is a cheetah, and he is Matthew's best friend.

The boys each gave Mom a kiss and a hug and hurried to catch up with Dad.

Once at camp, Matthew and Christopher separated from Michael and Grant. Michael and Grant headed for the junior leaders group. Matthew and Christopher headed for Coach Justin's group for the five- and six-year olds. Coach Justin is a puma and a very fast runner. The boys love him because he is so funny.

Coach Justin welcomed everyone and introduced the new campers to the group.

"We're going to have a great summer," said Coach Justin. "So let's start out with a soccer game."

Matthew and Christopher had a great morning. They each scored a couple of goals, and both played very good defense.

At lunch, Matthew saw Michael on the opposite side of the cafeteria and gave him a wave. Matthew was looking forward to free-play after lunch. Free-play was when Matthew was planning on climbing to the top of the jungle gym.

At the playground, Matthew and Christopher stood at the bottom of the jungle gym. They were looking straight up into the sky to the top.

"It looks like the top is in the clouds. It's a little too high for me to climb," said Christopher.

"Not me," said Matthew, and with that he started to climb. *First bar, easy,* Matthew thought. Matthew kept going. One arm then a leg, Matthew pulled himself up to the bar above him.

The horn blew for free-play to be over. The boys started to run over to Coach Justin.

"Come on down, Matthew!" shouted Christopher. "It's time to go back."

"I can't move, Christopher," said Matthew. "I'm frozen, and I can't move." Matthew was starting to get a little scared.

"I'm going to get Coach Justin for help!" Christopher yelled back. "Don't move."

"That won't be a problem," said Matthew as he held on to the bars so tightly that his hands were starting to hurt.

A few minutes later, Coach Justin and Michael came running up to the jungle gym. They wasted no time climbing up to Matthew.

"Hold on to me," said Coach Justin.

"I can't. I'm frozen!" cried Matthew.

"You will be safe, Matthew. Just grab on to Coach Justin," said Michael.

Matthew reached over to Coach Justin like he was told. The whole time, Michael kept talking to Matthew, reassuring him that he was safe.

That night at dinner, Matthew and Michael told their family the story of Matthew's jungle gym adventure.

"I'm so glad that you are safe and did not get hurt," said Mom, "Thank you, Michael, for helping your brother. I'm glad that you were there, and I'm very proud of you."

Michael blushed.

"Sounded like an exciting day," added Dad. "What are you going to do tomorrow at camp?"

Matthew thought about it a minute and then said, "I'm staying in the sandbox."

Everyone laughed.

MATTHEW TAKES
A NAP... OR NOT

It was Saturday, and Matthew woke up very early. He met his best friend, Christopher, at the park behind his house. They played soccer and baseball and even a little basketball. Matthew always had fun playing with Christopher.

Around lunchtime the boys said their good-byes, and each headed home. Matthew felt a little tired from all the activity and fresh air, but he was not about to take a nap. After all, he was five years old!

At the table at lunch, Matthew bothered his little sister. His mother had to speak to him twice about his behavior.

"Maybe you're a little tired from getting up so early and playing outside all morning. Fresh air always makes me sleepy," said Mom.

"I'm not sleepy, and I'm not grumpy, and I'm not going to take a nap!" snapped Matthew.

As soon as Matthew said that back to his Mom, he knew that he was in trouble.

"Sorry, Mom," said Matthew. But it was too late.

"Go up to your room, Matthew. I'll be up in a minute to talk with you," said Mom.

When Mom came in to his room, she sat at the end of his bed.

"Matthew, sometimes when people get tired, they get a little crabby. I know that you are five years old, but taking a nap is not just for babies. A nap helps you get back some energy to your body. You need to stay in your bed for one-half-hour because of your behavior. You do not have to sleep, but you might try just resting your eyes."

Matthew was determined not to go to sleep, so he held on to his stuffed toy lion, Rocky. Matthew watched the clock on his nightstand. It was one o'clock. He needed to stay in his bed until one thirty, and he was going to watch that clock every minute.

The next thing Matthew knew, it was four o'clock in the afternoon. He had been asleep for three whole hours!

Matthew ran downstairs. "I rested my eyes, and now I have so much energy!" he shouted.

"I see that," said Mom, smiling.

The rest of the day went great for Matthew. He played video games with Michael and ABC blocks with Madeline.

After dinner, Mom set up the Coconut Pickup game at the kitchen table. "Who wants to play?" called out Mom.

Matthew, Michael, and Madeline all came running into the kitchen and sat down at the table.

"Doesn't Dad want to play?" Mom asked.

"He can't right now," said Matthew. "He is resting his eyes and getting energy."

Everyone laughed.

MATTHEW
TRIES SOMETHING NEW

It was Thursday, and Matthew and his best friend Christopher were kicking the soccer ball around at the park behind Matthew's house. They were loving summer vacation.

"I have to leave soon," said Christopher. "We're going to Grandpa's house for dinner, and I told mom I would be home by three o'clock."

"That's okay," said Matthew. "I'm getting a little hungry anyway. My stomach just started to growl. I could use a snack. See you tomorrow." The boys waved good-bye.

When Matthew got home, he ran to the counter where the banana bread was this morning. It was not there.

"Mom, where is the banana bread?" asked Matthew.

"We finished it for lunch, remember?" said Mom. "Have something else."

When Matthew went to the fruit crate, there were no bananas or mangos.

"Mom, where are the bananas and mangos?" asked Matthew.

"They are all gone too, Matthew. I have them on my shopping list. Try something else," said Mom.

Matthew opened and closed the refrigerator three times. Matthew opened it again and just stared inside the refrigerator.

"Matthew, please don't leave the refrigerator door open. Just take something out and close the door," said Mom.

"There is nothing to eat," he said.

"There certainly is," added Mom. "There are blueberries."

"I don't like blueberries," said Matthew. "They are purplely blue, and I don't like to eat purplely blue food."

Mom just smiled.

"Berries, please?" said Madeline.

Mom put Madeline in her high chair. She put Madeline's bib on and gave her a handful of blueberries.

Matthew watched as Madeline ate the blueberries. He decided to just go to his room and wait for dinner.

He started to look at his library books, but his belly started to grumble. He decided to play with his racecars. He was so hungry. He could not concentrate. He had to get something to eat.

Matthew went into the kitchen where Madeline was playing with her dolls.

"Madeline," said Matthew, "did the blueberries taste good?"

"Mmm, berries," said Madeline.

Matthew went over to the refrigerator and took out a handful of berries. He looked at the blueberries, he smelled the blueberries, he took a deep breath, and he ate the blueberries.

Matthew had never tasted anything so sweet, juicy, and delicious before. Blueberries were great!

Matthew took out the whole container from the refrigerator, and he sat on the floor next to Madeline. Matthew and Madeline ate the rest of the blueberries.

Mom walked into the kitchen.

"What is going on?" she asked.

"Mmm, berries!" said Matthew and Madeline. Then they smiled at their mom with purplely blue smiles.

MATTHEW GETS A NEW NEIGHBOR

It was Friday, and Matthew was watching movers unload a big truck next door. His next-door neighbor, Mr. Lloyd, the sloth, had moved. Mr. Lloyd used to tell Matthew stories about trains, and Matthew was going to miss him. Mom had told him that Mr. Lloyd was getting older and moving a little slower. He was moving to live with his daughter and grandchildren in another jungle. Matthew was getting a new neighbor.

Matthew was very excited. He was hoping for someone he could play hide and seek with and maybe even some baseball. His brother Michael used to play with him, but lately Michael was hanging out with his friend, Grant. They did not always want Matthew around. So Matthew really wanted someone his own age to move in next door.

Matthew watched the movers unload the truck. There was a scooter. It was just about the size of the scooter that Matthew had. That was promising. The movers then unloaded a small bed. It was about the size of his bed. Matthew was getting very excited. But then the movers unloaded something that Matthew was not happy to see. Dolls! What? A girl was moving in next door. *Argh!* Matthew went to his room and stayed there the rest of the afternoon.

Later that night, Mom said, "Let's go over and welcome our new neighbors. I made some banana bread for them."

"You go," said Matthew. "I don't want to go."

"That is no way to act," Mom said. "Let's go."

The Adventures of Matthew the Monkey

Matthew was not happy but did what Mom had asked to do. They rang the doorbell. A nice lady giraffe answered the door. Matthew's mom introduced herself and Matthew.

The nice lady asked them to come in. Behind the nice lady, a little girl giraffe peeked around the corner.

"Elizabeth, come here and meet Matthew and his mom. She is a little shy around new people," said the nice lady to Mom.

Elizabeth came into the room. Elizabeth and Matthew each said hi to each other and then just stood there looking at each other not quite sure what to do next.

"Why don't you show Matthew your room?" said Elizabeth's mom.

Matthew did not want to go, but he knew he had to be polite. When they got to Elizabeth's room, Matthew was so surprised. There were so many books and puzzles and games. Matthew *loved* books and puzzles and games! Matthew noticed that Elizabeth had the game Coconut Pickup. This was one of Matthew's favorite games, and he was pretty good at it too. Matthew asked Elizabeth if she wanted to play a game of Coconut Pickup, and she said, "Yes." They played three games. Matthew won two games, and Elizabeth won one game. They had so much fun that Matthew was sad when his mom called him to go home.

"You can come back tomorrow," said Elizabeth's mom.

"Can I please?" Matthew asked Mom.

"Of course you can," said Mom.

Matthew smiled his very big smile all the way home.

Matthew thought to himself, *It might not be so bad having Elizabeth as a new next-door neighbor. Maybe I can even teach her to play baseball.*

MATTHEW
LEARNS TO READ

It was Friday, and summer vacation was just about over. Matthew and Michael had planned to do so much outside today, but it was raining. They were both going to play outside with their friends in the morning, and then Dad had taken a vacation day, and the family was going on a picnic in the afternoon. It looked like none of their plans were going to work out. What was Matthew going to do?

He looked around the house. Dad was reading the newspaper, and Mom was looking through her cookbooks for a new banana bread recipe. Madeline was playing with her ABC blocks, and Michael was reading a book about outer space he had just gotten from the library.

"Mom, what can I do today?" asked Matthew.

"Why don't you look at your new library books?" his mom replied.

"*But I don't know how to read!*" Matthew yelled. His mom gave Matthew the look that said to use his indoor voice.

"Sorry," said Matthew, quickly knowing that he should not have yelled in the house.

Mom said, "Why don't you look at the pictures in your books and try to figure out what the story is from the pictures, and I can read the story later."

"But I want you to read to me!" cried Matthew.

"Sorry, but I'm busy right now. Maybe later."

Matthew felt sad. He went to the living room, where Dad was reading the paper.

"Dad, will you read me a story?"

"Sorry, Matthew. I'm busy right now. Maybe later."

"That's what Mom said too," said Matthew.

Matthew felt even worse than before. He walked by Michael's bedroom.

"Michael, can you read to me?"

"Sorry, Matthew. I'm at a very interesting part of my book right now. Maybe later."

Matthew ran to his room and threw his library books on the bed and went back downstairs. He decided to play ABC blocks with Madeline. Madeline always loved it when Matthew played blocks with her. She loved her older brothers. Matthew usually loved playing with Madeline too, but today he was feeling a little frustrated.

His mom saw Matthew playing with Madeline and suggested that he use the ABC blocks to practice his letter sounds. Matthew just shrugged his shoulders a little.

His mom said, "You don't have to, but I want to thank you for playing with your sister so nicely."

Matthew smiled a little.

A little while later, Dad called out, "Hey, everyone, it stopped raining! Why don't we all go on that picnic we've been planning for today?"

"Great idea," said Mom. "I will pack a lunch for us with some mangos and the new banana bread I just made."

The family piled into the car and headed for the park. Once they were in the park, there were several roads that they could take. Dad stopped the car and asked, "Where should we go?"

Matthew said, "Let's go to the lake. Turn here."

Everyone turned and looked at Matthew.

"How did you know where the lake was?" asked Michael.

"I read it on the sign there. I sounded it out. Hey, wait a minute. *I can read! I read the sign!*" yelled Matthew.

Everyone clapped and cheered for Matthew, and he smiled his biggest smile ever.

It turned out to be a great day after all. Matthew had learned to read, and his mom's banana bread was delicious.

MATTHEW DOES NOT
TELL THE TRUTH

It was Saturday, and Matthew woke up smelling some wonderful smells coming from the kitchen. He sat up quickly, remembering it was Community Carnival Day, and he ran downstairs.

"The pies smell great!" said Matthew as he sat at the table. "You will win first prize for sure in the baking competition."

"Thank you, Matthew," answered Mom. "I'm only entering the fruit pie competition because your aunt Becca is entering her famous banana cream pie in the cream part of the competition. She is sure to take home first prize. Her pies are amazing."

"Now, Matthew," Mom continued. "Please stay away from the table. I don't want anything to happen to the pies. You may have your breakfast on the floor in the living room today."

Mom went upstairs to get ready for the carnival. Matthew ran into the kitchen to get some fruit for breakfast and slid across the floor to the refrigerator. He grabbed the fruit and slid back but lost his balance and slid right in to the table.

Matthew held his breath and looked at the pies. One of the pies had a cracked crust. He felt terrible. Matthew panicked and quickly ran outside to help Dad load the car for the carnival.

A few minutes later, they heard a scream from the kitchen. It was Matthew's mom. They both ran into the kitchen.

"What happened?" asked his Dad.

"I had my arms full when I came downstairs, and I bumped into the table. One of the pies crusts cracked," answered Mom.

"It's only one of them," said Matthew quietly.

"They judge on presentation," said his mom. "I was hoping to submit both. I should have been paying better attention."

Dad helped pack the good pie so that it would be safe and not crack while they were driving to the carnival. Everyone jumped into the car. They were very excited about the day ahead. They loved the carnival.

Community Carnival Days were held at Farmer Mark's farm. Farmer Mark is a water buffalo and a kind and gentle resident of Mango Grove. Every year, he opened his farm to the community to have the carnival there. It was so nice of him.

"I'm going to play every carnival game that they have there this year," said Michael.

"Eat banana!" said Madeline. She loved the caramel-covered bananas with peanuts sprinkled on top.

"How about you, Matthew?" asked Dad. "Are you going to try to dunk Coach Keith at the dunking booth?"

"I guess," said Matthew quietly.

"Are you all right? Do you feel okay?" asked Dad.

"I'm okay," answered Matthew.

As soon as they arrived, the family went to the pie-judging booth to watch Mom submit her pie. "It's hard to wait," said Mom. "I'm so nervous."

"Don't worry, Mom. You'll do great," said Michael.

"Your pie looked great," said Matthew timidly.

"Good luck," said Dad as he put his arm around Mom. The head judge came to the microphone to announce the winners.

No one was surprised that Aunt Becca had won first prize in the cream pie part of the competition. Second place was announced for the fruit pie part of the competition. It was Matthew's mom! Everyone cheered as she went up to get her ribbon. Farmer Mark was awarded the first-prize ribbon. He made an apple pie fresh from the apples in his orchard.

"Matthew, what is wrong?" asked Dad.

It all came spilling out. "I bumped into the table before Mom bumped into it, and I cracked her pie crust, not her. She may have won with the other pie that I wrecked!" cried Matthew. "I didn't tell a lie, I just did not say anything."

"But you didn't tell the truth either," said his dad. "It's the same as lying. Now go tell Mom so that we can all start having a good day."

Matthew went over and sat next to his mom. Matthew looked up at his mom with tears in his eyes. "I knocked into the table this morning before you knocked into it. I cracked the crust of your pie."

"I knew something was wrong. You were acting so differently," said Mom as she put her arm around Matthew.

"I'm sorry I didn't tell you the truth. I was afraid to tell you," said Matthew.

"Don't ever be afraid to tell the truth," said Mom. "You will always feel better about yourself when you choose not to lie. Your family and friends will know that you are trustworthy." Mom gave Matthew a little hug. "Come on. Let's join the others. Thank you for telling me about knocking into the table. I know that it was difficult for you."

Matthew and Mom walked back to the table holding hands and smiling. They had put the situation behind them.

"Now, let's start having some fun!" exclaimed Dad.

Madeline had a caramel-covered banana, Michael played every carnival game and won everyone a stuffed toy, and Matthew dunked Coach Keith three times at the dunking booth. They had such a great day.

At the end of the day, Mom spread out a blanket for a picnic. It was a perfect spot to watch the fireworks.

"Who wants pie?" asked Mom.

"We do!" everyone cried.

"This pie is delicious," said Matthew. "You should have won first prize today, Mom."

"I won first prize when I got this wonderful family," said his mom as she gave Matthew a hug.

MATTHEW
SLEEPS OVER

It was Monday, and Matthew, Mom, and Madeline were all out shopping. They were picking up a new sleeping bag for Matthew. On Saturday, he and Madeline were going overnight for a sleepover at their cousins' house. Matthew loved his cousins Wes, Jackson, and Carley, but he had never stayed overnight at their house before. He had never stayed overnight at anyone's house before. He was a little nervous. Mom and Dad were going to a wedding and would not be home until late, so his aunt and uncle offered to have Matthew and Madeline stay at their house. His brother Michael was staying at his friend Grant's house.

They had shopped at three stores so far, and Matthew had not found anything he liked.

"Only one more store left to look through. I hope that you find something that you like in here, or you may be out of luck," said Mom.

As they entered the store, Matthew saw the perfect bag.

"Great," said Mom. "Let me pay for it quickly before you change your mind."

That night, Matthew showed Dad his new sleeping bag. It was orange, his favorite color. On the inside was brown, and there was plenty of room for both Matthew and his stuffed toy lion Rocky.

As the week went on and it got closer to the sleepover, Matthew decided to talk to his brother. He was getting very nervous and needed a little reassurance.

"Michael, when you go overnight to Grant's house, do you get nervous?" asked Matthew.

"No way! Grant and I stay up and talk all night long. There's nothing to get nervous about."

"Okay, thanks," said Matthew, not really sure if he believed Michael.

When Matthew was in bed that night, he decided to try to stay awake all night, but he kept falling asleep. *Maybe I need someone to talk with,* he thought to himself. So he tried talking to Rocky, but Rocky did not have much to say. Matthew soon fell asleep.

Saturday morning was a tough one for Matthew. He was exhausted from trying to stay awake all night, and he almost fell asleep at the breakfast table.

"What is the matter with you this morning?" asked Mom.

Matthew told her about practicing staying awake like Michael does at Grant's house. Mom just smiled and gave Matthew a hug.

"You love your cousins, and Madeline will be there too. There is nothing to be nervous about. Now go up to your room and pack your suitcase so we can get going. And don't forget that new sleeping bag!"

Matthew did as he was told, and they were off driving to their cousin's house. Once they got there, Mom and Dad helped unload the car and then gave tons of kisses and hugs to Matthew and Madeline before they left. "We'll see you two in the morning," said Mom. "Have a good time with your cousins," said Dad.

Matthew noticed that Madeline was fine and that she and Carley took off down the hall to play. She did not seem nervous at all!

"Come on, Matthew!" yelled Wes and Jackson. "Let's play video games."

Matthew played all afternoon and really had a great time, but he kept thinking about the sleepover part. At dinner, Matthew was a little quiet, and his aunt asked him if he was okay. "Yes,

I'm fine," said Matthew. "It's pretty difficult to get a word in with everyone else talking so much." His aunt just smiled at him.

Later that night, the boys got to have popcorn and hot cocoa while his aunt put Carley and Madeline to bed. Madeline did not cry at all. *She is so brave*, thought Matthew.

At nine o'clock, his uncle said, "Okay, boys, time for bed."

Wes and Jackson shared a bedroom so all the boys would be together. The cousins had bunk beds. Wes slept on the top, and Jackson slept on the bottom bunk. Matthew was going to sleep on the floor in his sleeping bag next to the bunk beds.

"Cool sleeping bag," said Wes.

"Awesome bag," said Jackson.

The boys unrolled their bags too. Their dad had said that they could sleep in their sleeping bags because it was a special night with Matthew staying over. His aunt and uncle gave them each a kiss and said good night and turned off the light. Matthew squeezed his friend, Rocky, close to him.

"Want to talk all night long?" asked Matthew.

"No, thanks," said the boys. "We're kind of tired."

It was quiet for a while; then Matthew heard a noise.

"What's that?" asked Matthew.

"Just me," said Wes. "I came down to talk with you." Wes put his sleeping bag next to Matthew's bag on the floor. They talked a little bit, and then the boys heard another noise.

"What's that?" asked Matthew again.

"Just me," said Jackson. He was putting his sleeping bag on the other side of Matthew. "I wasn't going to let you two have all the fun."

The boys talked and talked and laughed and laughed, and Matthew had no idea what time it was when they finally all did fall asleep.

The next morning at breakfast, Matthew's aunt and uncle took a picture of Matthew and Wes and Jackson all asleep with their heads on the kitchen table next to their mango oatmeal.

MATTHEW
LEARNS ABOUT FRIENDSHIP

It was Saturday and the first day of a two-day baseball tournament. Matthew's team, the Tigers, was going to play the Jaguars.

Dad was driving Matthew and his best friend Christopher to the field. Christopher's dad was joining them later at the field. Christopher's dad was a doctor, and he had to first make a stop at the hospital to check on a few patients.

The boys were excited as they took their turns on the field to practice. Matthew played second base, and Christopher played shortstop. The twins, Eric and Ethan, and their cousin, Sam, all played the outfield. Coach Keith was hitting some balls out to the boys to get them warmed up.

Coach Keith was awesome. Matthew and his friends were so lucky to have had Coach Keith for two years in a row. He had played professional baseball, so he knew what he was talking about. Matthew and the team all paid very close attention when Coach was giving them instructions.

The game got started. The parents and families in the stands cheered for both teams. The boys were playing well, and the crowd clapped and encouraged them.

A ball rolled between Matthew's legs, but Christopher ran behind Matthew and saved the play! Another time, Matthew watched as Christopher dove for a fly ball and made a great catch.

Does Christopher ever make a mistake? Matthew thought to himself.

At bat, Matthew hit a double, a single, and struck out. Christopher hit two doubles and a home run.

The game was tied at two runs each. It was the Tigers' last chance to score. They were up to bat. Matthew was watching Christopher. The crowd was shouting, "Hit another home run, Christopher!"

Matthew found himself thinking a very strange thought. *If Christopher was not here, I would be the best player on the team.*

Just then, something horrible happened. Christopher was hit in the leg by a wild pitch. As he fell to the ground, he twisted his ankle.

Coach Keith and Christopher's dad ran out to help Christopher. They carefully picked him up and put him in their family car. His dad would take him to the hospital to check on his hurt ankle. Matthew could see that Christopher had been crying.

The Tigers ended up losing, three runs to two runs. The boys were all very worried about Christopher, and their minds were not on the game.

Later that evening at dinner, Matthew was very quiet. Mom encouraged him to try and eat something.

"I'm not hungry," said Matthew. "May I be excused?"

Matthew went to his room and sat on his bed. Soon after, Dad knocked on the door and asked if he could come in. Matthew nodded his head yes.

Dad put his arm around Matthew and said, "You know that Christopher will be okay. His dad is a doctor and will take good care of him."

"I know," said Matthew. "But I think that I was the one who got him hurt." Matthew explained to dad what he was thinking when Christopher got hurt.

His dad smiled and said, "I understand how you must be feeling. But first, you cannot hurt someone simply by thinking about it. Second, you seem to have a bit of the "jealousy bug.""

Dad went on to say, "Matthew, do you remember last summer when you scored all those goals during the soccer game and how at the end of the game Coach Justin awarded you with the most valuable player trophy?"

Matthew nodded.

"Well," he continued, "Do you remember what Christopher was doing when you scored all those goals and got that award?"

"He was cheering for me," said Matthew.

"Yes, because he is your friend, and he was happy for you."

"So, you are saying that I should be happy for someone when they are good at something?" said Matthew.

"Yes," said Dad, "especially if that person is your best friend. That's what friendship is all about."

The next day, everyone was so happy to see Christopher. He had his ankle wrapped, but he was okay to play baseball.

The second game was close again. The Tigers were winning, three runs to two runs. It was the bottom of the last inning. Matthew's team was in the field. They had to get one more out, and they would win the game.

The pitcher threw the ball. The batter was ready. He swung the bat, and the ball went flying. It was a great hit to the short-stop. Christopher readied himself, and he caught it. Christopher caught the ball! The Tigers had won the game! Everyone cheered.

The first one over to congratulate Christopher was Matthew. He now understood what it meant to be happy for a friend and what real friendship was all about.

MATTHEW
AND THE BIRTHDAY SURPRISE

It was Saturday, a very special Saturday. Today was Grandma Evelyn's sixtieth birthday. There was a big birthday party planned. Everyone was going to be there—all of Matthew's cousins and aunts and uncles too.

Grandma Evelyn and Matthew had a special bond. They loved spending time together. They had a special way of saying good-bye. Grandma Evelyn would stand on her front porch and wave and wave and wave until Matthew's family car was well out of sight. Matthew would be waving back to Grandma Evelyn until he couldn't see her house anymore. They both agreed that the longer they waved, the more love would come their way.

"Mom, I want to give Grandma Evelyn something special for her birthday," said Matthew.

"We already have some very nice things for her," said Mom. "We have a pair of sweatpants and a sweatshirt. They are purple, her favorite color."

"No, I want something special just from me," said Matthew.

"You can give her some daisies from the yard."

"No, not that," said Matthew. "I'll figure it out."

"You need to hurry then," said Mom. "We are leaving in an hour."

Matthew went outside to look around. Grandma Evelyn loved butterflies. He could try to catch a butterfly for her. While Matthew was looking up in the sky for a butterfly, he did not notice a stone in the path, and he tripped and fell.

He did not get hurt, but as he was getting up from the ground, he got a great idea. Matthew ran back into the house and asked Mom for some tissue paper and a ribbon.

A few minutes later, Matthew and his family were headed for Grandma Evelyn's house for the party. The party was in full swing when they got there, and it was so much fun seeing everyone.

"Time to open presents!" yelled Matthew's dad. Everyone gathered around. Grandma Evelyn *oohed* and *ahhed* as she opened her gifts. She gave kisses and hugs and thanked everyone for coming.

Matthew walked over to Grandma Evelyn and gave her a small package. "This is just from me," said Matthew.

Grandma Evelyn opened the present. It was an oval-shaped piece of play-sand with a handprint on it.

"It's my hand," said Matthew. "When you look at it, you can think of me waving to you and sending you love."

Grandma Evelyn hugged Matthew and whispered in his ear, "This is the best gift I have ever received. I love you."

That night when Matthew and his family left the party and drove away, Matthew waved to Grandma Evelyn for an extra-long time. He knew in his heart that she was waving back too. He knew because they had that special bond.

MATTHEW
GETS LOST

It was Saturday, the Saturday before school started, and Matthew and Mom were going shopping at the public market and then out to breakfast. It was so nice to have special alone time with his mom.

Matthew got changed quickly and ran downstairs to the kitchen. Mom and Dad were sitting at the kitchen table drinking their coffee. Madeline was in her highchair eating some blueberries.

"Mmm, berries," said Madeline.

"Morning," said Matthew as he popped a couple of berries into his mouth.

"Good morning, Matthew," said his mom. "Are you ready to get going?"

"I sure am," said Matthew.

Matthew gave Dad and Madeline a kiss and helped take the cloth shopping bags to the car for Mom. On their way to the market, Matthew and Mom talked and talked. They talked about Matthew's new school year and his baseball team. They talked about the new recipes Mom was going to try to make this week. They enjoyed each other's company.

When they got to the market, Mom found a great parking spot close to the banana man. Matthew loved the banana man! As soon as he got out of the car, he could hear him yelling.

"Banana, banana, banana, get your bananas!"

It always made Matthew smile when he heard the banana man's cry.

Before going into the market, Mom gave Matthew "the speech." Mom looked at Matthew and said, "Matthew, remember to stay close to me. Do you remember why it's so important for you to do that?"

"Yes, Mom. It's because we might get separated, and I might get lost," said Matthew.

"That's right. Do you remember what happens if we do get separated?"

"I go to the banana man's stand," said Matthew.

"Yes, that's good, but what happens if you can't find the banana man's stand?"

"I find a safe person and ask them for help," said Matthew.

"Perfect!" said Mom. "Let's get shopping."

They went into the market. It was buzzing with lots of people, lots of music, and lots of wonderful smells.

Matthew and Mom picked up some mangos and blueberries. Out of the corner of his eye, Matthew saw people gathering around someone. Matthew moved a little closer and saw a chef cooking some pancakes. He was flipping the pancakes over by tossing them high up in the air and then catching them in the pan. Everyone clapped.

"That was awesome, wasn't it, Mom?" Matthew asked, looking up at the lady next to him. The lady next to him smiled, but it was not his mom.

Matthew became a little nervous. He looked around a little but did not see his mom.

Matthew remembered "the speech." He remembered what he should do if they got separated. He was supposed to meet Mom at the banana man's table. Matthew was not sure which way to go to get to the banana man's table.

He tried to listen for the "banana, banana" song, but it was so noisy that he could not hear the song. Matthew looked around again and saw a policeman. He knew that he could talk to a policeman because a policeman was a safe person.

Matthew walked over to the policeman. "Excuse me," said Matthew, "I cannot find my mom, and I'm supposed to meet her

at the banana man's table if we get separated, but I don't know where it is because I'm too short."

Policeman Bob smiled and took Matthew's hand. "Come on, the table is right over there. I will go with you." Policeman Bob is a honey badger, and he put Matthew at ease.

As Matthew and Policeman Bob got closer to the table, Matthew saw Mom. Mom saw Matthew at the same time. They both ran into each other's arms. They hugged and hugged and hugged.

"Thank you so much for helping Matthew," said Mom to the policeman.

Policeman Bob said, "You're welcome. Matthew was very brave, and he did the right thing by asking me for help."

At breakfast later that morning, Matthew said, "Mom, you should have seen the chef today. He was flipping the pancakes high in the air and catching them. It was so cool."

"I bet it was. Sorry that I missed it," said Mom.

Matthew added, "I'm sorry that I wasn't paying attention and that we got separated."

Mom smiled and said, "All that matters now is that you're safe. I'm very proud of you for being so brave today."

Their breakfast was served. Banana pancakes.

As they picked up their forks, they both said, "Banana, banana, banana, get your bananas!"

MATTHEW MAKES
A GOOD DECISION

It was Monday, and the first week of school had flown by. Matthew loved seeing his friends again. His teacher, Miss Nina, was so nice. Miss Nina is an African gray parrot and one of the smartest parrots Matthew had ever met. He was going to enjoy this school year.

Matthew and Mom were filling a box with items from a list that Miss Nina had sent home. Matthew had learned in school that day that Miss Nina knew a family whose house had burned down, and they needed to replace everything. Miss Nina's class wanted to help, so they were collecting items from the list.

Matthew had donated some of his puzzles, and his sister Madeline put one of her baby dolls in the box. Mom had found some clothes that the family had outgrown and added them to the box. Dad added some tools, and even Michael threw in a couple of his favorite comic books.

"Great job," said Mom. "Now, Matthew, finish your chores, and get ready for bed."

Matthew ran down to the kitchen to clear the table from dinner. Matthew was saving his allowance for a new video game. He wanted to get the new car-racing video game. Matthew loved car racing. He watched it on TV any chance he got and pretended he was a famous racecar driver.

"I have six dollars saved so far, and the video game costs fifteen dollars. How much more do I need, Michael?" asked Matthew.

Michael was great at math. Matthew always asked him for help when he had a math problem to solve.

"You need nine more dollars," answered Michael.

"It seems to be taking forever," said Matthew.

"It will be worth the wait," said Mom from the doorway. "Because you will appreciate it so much more because you earned it."

The next morning at the bus stop, Matthew and his friends Christopher and Elizabeth were all carrying boxes for the needy family. They were talking about the items they were donating.

The school bus stop was located right next to the city bus stop, so in the morning it was a busy street with children waiting for their school bus and other older people waiting for the city bus to get to work.

Matthew looked over and watched the grownups getting on the city bus. He saw something drop out of a man's pocket. Matthew ran over to pick it up and yelled out, "Sir, you dropped something!" It was too late. The man had gotten on the bus, and the door had closed. Matthew had to run to get back to his stop and get on the bus.

When he sat down on the bus next to Christopher, he looked down in his hand.

"Wow, it is a ten-dollar bill. With this money, I would have more than enough to buy that new racing game!" exclaimed Matthew.

Matthew thought about the money in his pocket all day. Miss Nina had to ask him to please pay attention on several occasions.

That night, after Dad had finished reading a bedtime story, Matthew told his dad about the money.

"Well, Matthew, the money is not yours. You should try to return it to the man who dropped it. Let's say if the man is not at the bus stop the rest of the week, you may do what you want with the money," said his dad. *That seemed fair,* thought Matthew as he drifted off to sleep.

The next morning at the bus stop, Matthew looked around at the grownups, and he saw the man who had dropped the money. He was a little disappointed that the man was there because he really would have liked to keep the money, but he knew he had to make the right decision. Matthew walked over to the man.

"Excuse me, sir, but yesterday you dropped this getting on the bus," Matthew said as he handed the man the ten-dollar bill.

"You are a very honest boy. Your parents must be very proud of you. Thank you, and as a reward, you make keep the money and use it however you like," said the man.

Matthew smiled and put the money in his pocket and started to daydream about the car-racing video game.

When Matthew sat down for dinner that night, to his surprise there was a small bag at his plate. He opened the bag, and inside was the car-racing video game that he had wanted so much.

Mom said, "Miss Nina called today and told us that you donated the ten dollars to the family in need. That was an amazing thing to do. Your dad and I thought that you deserved something special for that good decision."

"Thanks, Mom and Dad," said Matthew.

"Now that you have the car-racing video game, what are you going to be saving your allowance for?" asked Michael

"Car racing, the road course video game!" said Matthew.

Mom and Dad just shook their heads and smiled.

MATTHEW
GETS A PET

It was Friday, and Matthew was very excited. He was going to watch his friend Christopher's puppy. Christopher and his family were going out of town overnight. Matthew was going to puppy-sit.

Matthew had been asking his mom and dad for a puppy for a long time. Mom said that watching Christopher's puppy would be good practice. She also said it would teach Matthew responsibility.

Matthew had made a place for Christopher's puppy to sleep right next to his bed. Mom had even let Matthew get a little squeaky toy for the puppy.

The time had finally arrived, and Christopher and his dad pulled into the yard with their puppy. Christopher's dad brought in the puppy's bed, the puppy's food, and some puppy toys. Christopher brought in the puppy.

Matthew and his family gathered around Christopher, who introduced them to his puppy, Milton. He gave some last-minute instructions to Matthew, kissed Milton good-bye, and left with his dad.

Matthew and his family sat on the floor around Milton. They took turns petting and holding Milton.

Soon after, Mom got up and took Madeline in for her bath. His dad also got up saying he had to finish reading the newspaper. Michael got up too. He said he wanted to play video games.

Matthew was left alone with Milton.

"Dad, what do I do now?" asked Matthew.

"Maybe you should take Milton for a walk before it gets dark," suggested Dad.

"Good idea," said Matthew. "Come on, Milton."

Matthew hooked up Milton's leash to his collar and took him outside. Halfway down the street, Milton just sat down. He refused to budge. He would not go any farther.

"Come on, Milton," pleaded Matthew. No matter what he tried, Milton refused to move.

Matthew decided to pick Milton up and carry him home. Milton was not so heavy when Matthew first picked him up, but by the time he got home, Matthew's arms were getting a little sore because Milton was getting heavy.

After dinner that evening, Matthew's mom reminded him to feed the puppy and make sure that he had fresh water.

Milton gobbled his food and ended up spilling his water. Matthew grabbed a towel and cleaned up the puppy's mess.

On Friday nights, Matthew and his family usually watch a movie together. But on this particular Friday night, Matthew was not able to enjoy the movie. He had to keep jumping up and checking on Milton. He was getting into so many things.

First, he got into the garbage. Then Milton got into Mom's clean laundry. Matthew had to help refold the whole laundry basket. And worst of all, Milton took Matthew's favorite stuffed toy lion, Rocky. Matthew did not like that one bit.

"Why doesn't he play with his own toys?" asked Matthew. "He's getting into everything."

Finally, it was time for bed. Matthew was exhausted. He put Milton in to his bed and crawled into his own bed. Right after Matthew fell asleep, Milton started to cry. He woke Matthew up three times. Matthew ended up taking his pillow and blanket and lying on the floor next to Milton to keep him from crying.

The next morning, Matthew was very tired.

"You had better take the puppy out before he has an accident in the house," Mom said.

"I will," said Matthew. This is not what he wanted to do, but he really did not want to have to clean up a mess if Milton had an accident in the house.

Christopher and his dad stopped by to pick up Milton around four o'clock. As Christopher hugged Matthew, he said, "Thank you so much, Matthew, for watching Milton. I hope that he was not too much trouble for you."

"No," said Matthew. "Milton was fine."

On Sunday afternoon, Dad said, "Matthew, would you like to go to the pet store. You have proven to me and your mom that you are very responsible. You deserve to have a puppy."

"Sure, Dad," said Matthew. "But I've been thinking I want to get a goldfish instead."

MATTHEW
EARNS A MERIT BADGE

It was Saturday. Mom was sewing Matthew's latest merit badge to his scout sash. Since school had started, Matthew joined the monkey scouts and was really enjoying earning merit badges. Matthew had three badges so far—the sports badge, the hiking badge, and the science badge. He was now working on his career badge.

In order to achieve the career badge, Matthew had to interview five adults and ask them about their careers, and then Matthew had to write a paragraph about each career. So far, Matthew had interviewed his baseball coach, Coach Keith; his friend Christopher's dad, who is a doctor; his teacher, Miss Nina; and his uncle Brian, who drives the school bus.

"I need one more interview, and I want to balance it a little, so I need a girl," said Matthew.

"How about Mom?" asked Matthew's dad.

"She doesn't work," said Matthew.

"She certainly does," said Dad.

Just then, they heard a terrible noise and heard Mom call out, "Help, I twisted my ankle."

Matthew and Dad ran out to the backyard. Mom had twisted her ankle going down the back steps.

"Looks like you should stay off your feet today," said Dad. "I was going to stop by work a little later this morning, but I can cancel and stay home to help out."

"No, Dad," said Matthew, "I will help out. This way I can see the work that Mom does because I will be helping."

"Okay, I won't be long. You have my number at work if you need me."

Michael came into the living room.

"Mom, can I have a ride to the library this afternoon? Hey, what happened?"

"Your mom twisted her ankle. If you want a ride to the library, we would have to leave now. I can drop you off on my way to work."

After his dad and Michael had left, Matthew asked his mom what he could do to help.

"Just hand me your sash, and I will finish sewing on your sports badge," said his mom. "And I would love a piece of the banana bread that I made this morning. Thank you."

When Matthew came back with the banana bread, he noticed that his mom had finished sewing on the badge and was reading a story to his sister, Madeline.

"More stories," said Madeline.

"Go ahead to your room and get another story," said his mom to Madeline.

As Madeline ran down the hallway, she tripped and scraped her knee. She ran crying back to Mom.

"Matthew, could you get a wash cloth and a bandage for me, please?" asked Mom as she rocked Madeline.

Matthew did as he was told, and he watched as mom cleaned Madeline's booboo and gave it a kiss to help it heal quickly.

"Time for a nap," she said to Madeline. "You go with Matthew, and he will tuck you in."

After tucking Madeline in, Matthew went to the kitchen to continue working on his career badge paragraphs.

Soon afterward, Dad came home from work and walked over to Matthew in the kitchen. "What did you decide about your fifth interview?" asked Dad.

"I decided that I only have to interview Mom for my whole badge," said Matthew. "She is a cook, a seamstress, a driver, a librarian, a doctor, and a whole lot more. Dad, she works hard!"

Dad smiled and said, "Yes, she does, Matthew. Yes, she does."

MATTHEW
CLEANS UP

It was Sunday afternoon. Matthew and Michael were finishing up their homework and putting things that they needed for school the next day in their backpacks. Mom always wanted the boys to be prepared.

"This way," she would say, "no one is running around looking like crazy for something on Monday morning."

This coming week was special. Matthew was student of the week. Being student of the week, Matthew was able to bring something special for show and tell to class and talk about it. Matthew knew right away what that something special was going to be.

Matthew had a rookie card of his baseball coach, Coach Keith. Coach Keith is a fox, and Matthew really admired him. Coach had played professional baseball, and his rookie card was one of Matthew's prized possessions.

Matthew went to his room to get the card to pack in his backpack. When he got to his room, he was not quite sure where he had put the card.

Also, Matthew's room was very, very messy. Matthew was not sure where to start looking for his card.

"Mom, do you know where my Coach Keith card is?" asked Matthew.

"No, I don't know where you keep it," answered Mom as she came into Matthew's room. "Matthew, your room is a mess. No wonder you can't find anything. You need to clean up."

"But I need the card for tomorrow!" cried Matthew.

"Then you had better get started," said his mom. "Inch by inch."

Matthew did not like when his mom said that. It usually meant that Matthew had a lot of work to do.

Matthew took a deep breath and started to sort through the mess. He thought about what Mom would say. "Inch by inch" simply meant that a little at a time and the project will get done.

Matthew picked up all his blocks and put them in his toy chest. He then put all his books back on the shelf. Matthew worked all afternoon, and when everything was put back where it belonged, Matthew still had not found his Coach Keith card.

Matthew came downstairs to the kitchen, sat at the table, and started to cry.

"What's wrong, Matthew?" asked Dad.

Matthew explained about cleaning up his room and needing the card for show and tell the next day at school. Matthew was so upset. Dad had taken the next day as a vacation day and promised that he would look again tomorrow for the card while Matthew was in school.

Matthew did not sleep well that night. He had decided to take his stuffed toy lion, Rocky, for show and tell. He loved Rocky, but almost everyone had seen him already.

The next day at school while Matthew was in class, there was a knock on the classroom door. Miss Nina flew over to answer the door. She spoke to the person at the door for a while. Miss Nina came back in to the room.

"Matthew," said Miss Nina, "I think now is a good time for your show and tell."

Matthew got up from his seat and headed toward his backpack to get Rocky.

"I think you wanted to talk about this," said Miss Nina.

Matthew looked up and saw Coach Keith standing next to Miss Nina.

"Coach!" shouted Matthew. He ran to the front of the room.

"Your dad called and said that you misplaced my rookie card. I brought you another one. Don't lose this one," said Coach Keith as he handed Matthew the card.

"I won't," said Matthew. He had a great show and tell that day. He told the class about the card, and he had the real Coach Keith with him too. That was such a treat for Matthew and the class.

Later that evening, Matthew thanked Dad for calling Coach Keith. Matthew also apologized to both Mom and Dad for having such a messy bedroom.

"Remember, Matthew," said his dad, "you may not be so lucky next time. If you misplace something again, it may be gone forever."

"I know," said Matthew. "I promise to keep my room clean from now on. Little by little, inch by inch."

MATTHEW
"ON HIS OWN" DAY

It was Saturday. Matthew and his best friend Christopher were at the park behind Matthew's house, watching the clouds.

"That one looks like a lion," said Matthew.

"It sure does," said Christopher. "And those look like a bunch of balloons. I wish we could do this all day long, but I have to get home for lunch. Talk to you tomorrow."

The boys said their good-byes, but Matthew stayed at the park. He knew it was almost time for lunch, but he did not care, and he did not go home.

After another hour went by, Matthew headed home.

"Where were you?" asked Mom. "You missed lunch, and I was getting worried."

"I wasn't hungry," said Matthew.

"You need to come home for lunch," said Dad. "Those are the rules."

Matthew just made a face.

His mom added, "Matthew, please get washed up. We are headed for Grandma Evelyn's house. She has not been feeling well, and I made some soup for her."

"Why do we all have to go?" asked Matthew.

"Because we are a family, and that's what families do. We help each other," said Dad.

That evening at bedtime, Matthew's mom kissed Matthew good night and asked, "Why were you a little crabby today? You usually love going to see Grandma Evelyn."

"I'm tired of rules. I'm tired from going to school every day. I'm tired of helping people, and I'm tired of people bugging me," said Matthew.

"Well, maybe you will feel better tomorrow," said Mom.

The next morning, Matthew jumped out of bed. Sunday was his favorite day. His dad made his famous banana and blueberry waffles for breakfast for everyone. But when Matthew got to the kitchen, no one was there. They were all in the backyard playing in the sprinkler.

"Hey, where are the waffles?" yelled Matthew out the back door.

"We already ate," said Mom. "We decided you can have a 'Just Matthew Day' so you are on your own. There is plenty to eat in the refrigerator. Help yourself."

"Yahoo!" said Matthew as he helped himself to a banana. It wasn't waffles, but it would do.

Matthew decided to play his favorite car-racing video game. It was exciting at first, but after a while, he got very tired of playing the game by himself.

Matthew looked outside and saw his family having a picnic lunch. They were all laughing and having a good time. Matthew was a little hungry, so he grabbed another banana and headed to his room.

He decided to call his friend Elizabeth to see if she wanted to come over to play their favorite board game Coconut Pickup. Elizabeth was not home. Matthew tried playing the game alone, but that definitely was not fun. So he decided to get his homework done.

Matthew started with his math problems, but they were so hard that Matthew needed to ask his brother Michael for help. Michael was so good at math, and he always helped Matthew understand the math problems and how to reach a solution.

Matthew was surprised when he asked Michael for help. "I can't help you today. It's 'Just Matthew Day' so you are on your own," said Michael.

Matthew went back to the TV room, and since there were no rules today, Matthew turned up the volume on the TV. No one said anything to him, and he soon became bored.

He grabbed another banana and went to his room and took a nap. When Matthew woke up, he smelled the delicious smell of pizza coming from the kitchen. He jumped out of bed and ran down to the kitchen and saw Michael eating the last piece of pizza.

Matthew had had it. "Hey, what about me?" Matthew asked with tears in his eyes. This "Just Matthew Day" was not at all what he expected.

"I'm sorry. I want to be part of the family. I want rules, and I want to help. I want you to help me too," cried Matthew.

Matthew's family surrounded him and gave him lots of hugs and kisses.

"I will help you with your math homework," said Michael.

"Okay, thanks. But first, I'm a little hungry," said Matthew.

"I will make you some banana and blueberry waffles," added Dad.

Matthew said, "Thanks, Dad. I love you, but could you please leave out the bananas on those waffles?"

MATTHEW
AND A NEW TRADITION

It was Monday. Matthew and his family were all sitting around the breakfast table staring at their mango oatmeal.

"It's so hard to get started on Mondays," said Matthew.

"You're right," added Dad. "I know that I'll have a ton of work waiting for me when I get to the office, and I'm not looking forward to it."

"I always have so much laundry from the weekend to do," said Mom. "And if I have any extra energy, I like to start my baking for the week."

"We need something to look forward to on Mondays to help get us through the day," said Matthew.

"The only thing I have to look forward to is homework," added Michael.

"That is a great idea you have, Matthew," said Mom. "We will all have to give this a little thought and try to come up with something."

"But for now, we need to get going," said Dad.

Matthew's dad left for work, and his mom started her first load of laundry. Matthew and Michael grabbed their backpacks, gave Mom a kiss, and headed out the door to their bus stop.

Monday had officially started.

At the bus stop, Matthew spoke to his friends Christopher and Elizabeth about how hard it was to get going on Mondays. They agreed with Matthew and thought that his idea about looking forward to something would definitely help the day along.

Matthew's Monday turned out to be worse than he expected. He had a surprise math test in class, and he was not very prepared. At lunch, he dropped his tray. At recess, he tripped and scraped his knee.

"Mondays are the pits," said Matthew as he and his friends boarded the bus to go home. "At least it's almost over."

After getting off the bus, Matthew and Michael started walking to their home. They saw Mom, Dad, and Madeline sitting on the front steps.

"What's going on?" asked Matthew.

"Hop in the car, and we will explain," said their mom.

The boys did as they were told.

"Matthew, Mom and I were talking today about your idea from this morning. We think we may have come up with something," said his dad.

Matthew's dad drove up to their favorite restaurant drive-thru and ordered four large mango shakes. Matthew and Michael smiled at each other, and little Madeline clapped her hands.

Dad then drove to a park close by, and Mom spread out a blanket and passed out the shakes. Mom shared her shake with Madeline.

"This is awesome! Can we do this every Monday?" asked Matthew.

"Yes," said Mom. "It can be a new tradition. We will call it Mango Shake Monday."

"Yahoo!" shouted everyone.

Matthew's family shared stories about their day then headed home. They all agreed Mango Shake Monday was a great success.

"Hey, everyone," said Matthew, "how about Tropical Smoothie Tuesday?"

Everyone laughed, and Mom and Dad just shook their heads.

MATTHEW
TAKES A FIELD TRIP

It was Wednesday. Matthew and his class were on the field trip bus headed for Farmer Mark's. He is larger than life to the children. He is the most kind and gentle water buffalo you would ever want to meet. The kids loved him. Farmer Mark had an amazing place. It was where the community had their carnival every summer. The farm had animals and a peach and an apple orchard. There was so much to see. The class was promised a hayride too.

As the bus pulled into the driveway, the class could see Farmer Mark waving to them. They could also hear his two dogs, Millie and Mason, barking their hellos.

Farmer Mark had the tractor and trailer all hooked up and ready for the hayride. Matthew and his class hopped on the trailer. Millie and Mason hopped on the trailer too. They had not stopped barking; they were so happy to see the kids. Millie and Mason sat next to the twin elephants, Ethan and Eric.

Ethan and Eric were Matthew's friends. They were twins and looked exactly alike, and it was very difficult at times to tell them apart. That was okay because they were always together anyway.

Farmer Mark picked Matthew's friend Christopher to help him drive the tractor. Matthew thought that he would have loved getting picked for that. He would love to drive a tractor.

When the class got to the apple orchard, Farmer Mark parked the tractor. The class had an opportunity to pick apples. It was great fun, and the apples were delicious. Matthew's friend

Elizabeth was chosen to have a ride in the apple bucket. She was able to pick an apple higher up on the tree. Matthew thought what fun that would be to take a ride in the bucket and how lucky Elizabeth was to have been picked to go for a ride.

The class finished their apples and got back on the trailer. They headed back to the barn. The field trip was almost over. Only one more stop to see the pigs and cows.

Matthew was enjoying himself, but he was beginning to feel a little jealous because his friends had all been picked to do something special. Christopher drove the tractor, Elizabeth got a ride in the apple bucket, and even Eric and Ethan were having a special time with the dogs, Millie and Mason.

At the cow barn, Farmer Mark showed the class how to milk a cow. It was a fascinating process.

"Matthew," said Farmer Mark, "would you like to try to milk a cow?"

"I sure would!" exclaimed Matthew. Matthew was a little nervous because the cow was so big. He remembered what Farmer Mark had showed the class about milking a cow, and he repeated the process. Matthew heard the milk in the bucket and the class cheered. He did it! Matthew had milked a cow!

Back in the classroom, Miss Nina asked the class to draw a picture of their best memory from the field trip. Christopher drew a picture of the tractor. Elizabeth drew a picture of the apple bucket. Eric and Ethan both drew a picture of the dogs, Millie and Mason—their pictures even looked the same. Matthew knew right away what he was going to draw. It was a picture of himself milking the cow.

That evening at dinner, Matthew told his family all about the field trip and showed them the picture. Mom and Dad were so proud of Matthew that the picture went to a place of honor, right on the refrigerator.

"Moo, moo," said Madeline, and everyone laughed.

"Moo, moo," they all said.

MATTHEW
VISITS A HOSPITAL

It was Thursday and two weeks before Thanksgiving. When Matthew woke up, he knew right away something was wrong. His throat really hurt when he swallowed.

Matthew went downstairs to the kitchen where Mom was getting breakfast ready for everyone.

"Mom, my throat hurts," whispered Matthew.

"Again?" said Mom. "This is the third time this month. I will make an appointment with the doctor this morning. You go lie down on the couch. No school for you today."

Mom was able to make an appointment for Matthew at eleven that morning. Matthew liked his doctor. The doctor was his best friend Christopher's dad.

At the appointment, the doctor looked at Matthew's throat and knew right away that Matthew needed to have his tonsils removed. Matthew's mom agreed.

"I have someone scheduled for ten tomorrow, and I can fit Matthew in right after that," said the doctor.

"Perfect," said mom. "This way he will be feeling great for the holidays."

That night, Mom and Dad explained to Matthew that they would be going to the hospital tomorrow and that Matthew would be having his tonsils removed.

"Will it hurt?" asked Matthew.

"Not any more than your throat hurts now," said Dad. "And the cool part is that you will get lots of ice cream, even for dinner."

"Yahoo!" shouted Matthew as he grabbed his throat. He needed to remember not to shout because it hurt his throat.

The next day at the hospital, Matthew and his mom and dad were shown to the room that Matthew would be staying in.

Nurse Megan came in and introduced herself. She was the nicest zebra. "I will be staying with you the whole time that you are here, Matthew. If you need anything, don't hesitate to ask," said Nurse Megan. "I will also be checking in on the person in the bed next to you. He is my patient too." She pulled back the curtain.

"What are you doing here?" asked Matthew to the man in the next bed.

"Having my tonsils out. What are you doing here?" asked the man in the next bed.

To his surprise, Matthew saw his old neighbor, Mr. Lloyd. Mr. Lloyd used to live next door to Matthew until he moved away to live with his daughter.

The two friends laughed about being in the same room and getting their tonsils out at the same time. They talked and talked. Mr. Lloyd told Matthew some new stories about trains, and Matthew told Mr. Lloyd about his friend Elizabeth who had moved into Mr. Lloyd's old house.

Nurse Megan came in with a wheelchair. "Time to go, Mr. Lloyd," said Nurse Megan. "I will be back for you in a minute, Matthew."

When Nurse Megan returned, Matthew kissed Mom and Dad and went for a ride in the wheelchair.

After the operation, both Mr. Lloyd and Matthew said that their throats were sore.

"I know what will help," said Nurse Megan. "I will be right back."

Nurse Megan returned with two great big bowlfuls of banana ice cream.

Matthew and Mr. Lloyd dug in to their ice cream and smiled. It felt so good on their sore throats.

"Getting your tonsils out isn't too bad," said Matthew. "Let's do it again next year."

Everyone just laughed while Matthew and Mr. Lloyd finished eating their banana ice cream.

MATTHEW AND THANKSGIVING LOVE

It was Wednesday and the day before Thanksgiving. Mom was putting some last-minute additions on her shopping list.

Matthew came running in from outside. "Mom, can I come shopping with you?" he asked.

"Of course. Let's get going. We have plenty to do," answered Mom.

On the way to the grocery store, Matthew said, "Mom, Elizabeth and her mom are going to be by themselves for Thanksgiving. Can they come to our house? You always say Thanksgiving is about who you love and who loves you."

Mom smiled and said, "Yes, I think that is a good idea. I'll call Elizabeth's mom when we get home."

The grocery store was so busy. Matthew stayed close to his mom. He did not want to get separated from her like the day at the public market.

At the deli counter, Matthew and Mom ran into Coach Justin and Coach Keith.

"Would you two stay with Matthew while I run down this aisle to pick up some peanuts?" asked Mom.

"Of course. Go ahead," said Coach Justin.

When Mom came back to the cart, she was a little surprised when Coach Keith said, "Matthew has invited Coach Justin and I for Thanksgiving dinner tomorrow. We would love to come, if that's okay with you."

"Um, sure," said Mom. "Stop by around two o'clock."

"I'm dating Nurse Megan. Would it be okay if I bring her too?" asked Coach Keith.

"Sure. How about you, Coach Justin. Would you like to bring someone too?" asked Mom.

"No, I'm good. Just me," he answered.

Matthew and Mom said their good-byes and finished their shopping.

"Matthew, please don't invite people over without first checking with me," said Mom.

"Sorry, Mom," said Matthew.

When Matthew and Mom pulled in to the yard, Dad ran to help unload the groceries from the car.

"What are we feeding, an army?" asked Dad.

"Just about," answered Matthew's mom.

"Oh, I ran into Mr. Lloyd at the fish and tackle shop today. He said that he was going to be alone tomorrow, so I invited him over," said Dad.

Matthew and Mom just looked at each other.

Mom sat at the table with a pencil and paper.

"I have got to add up how many people will be here tomorrow.

1. *Mom*
2. *Dad*
3. *Matthew*
4. *Michael*
5. *Madeline*
6. *Aunt Becca*
7. *Uncle Brian*
8. *Carley*
9. *Wes*
10. *Jackson*
11. *Grandma Evelyn*
12. *Elizabeth*
13. *Elizabeth's mom*
14. *Mr. Lloyd*
15. *Coach Justin*

Seventeen! Where will we put everyone?" exclaimed Mom.
"We'll manage," answered Dad.

Thanksgiving Day finally arrived. The house was filled with
wonderful smells. People arrived and laughed and talked with
each other. It was a perfect day.

Everyone was a little squished when they sat down, but no
one complained. The food was delicious. Mom received a round
of applause for preparing such an amazing feast.

Matthew looked up at Dad and said, "A lot of love, here in
this house."

Dad bent down and hugged Matthew.

"Yes, Matthew. A lot of love."

MATTHEW'S
CHRISTMAS ADVENTURE

It was Tuesday and two days before Christmas. Matthew and his family were stringing popcorn and cranberries to decorate the family Christmas tree.

"This pattern looks great!" said Matthew. "Two pieces of popcorn, then two cranberries, then repeat."

"Yes, it does look great," said Mom, "You are doing a wonderful job."

"Let's finish this up a little later," said Dad. "We're due at the Community Center soon to help set up for the Christmas day dinner and celebration."

"Dad, does the center have a Christmas tree yet?" asked Michael.

"Yes, Coach Justin got one the other day, but no decorations yet," answered Dad.

"Let's take what we have here to the center, and we can make more tonight for our tree," suggested Matthew.

"Great idea," said Mom. "I have a box in the garage we can put everything in."

Mom and Dad loaded the car, and the family piled in and headed for the community center.

The community center was run by Coach Keith and Nurse Megan. Matthew and his family volunteered there as much as they could. Mom was always baking extra so she could donate to the community pantry located at the center.

When they arrived at the center, Coach Keith and Nurse Megan came out to help unload the car. Coach Keith gave

Matthew a high four, and Nurse Megan game him a hug. Matthew always blushed a little when she did that, but he had to get used to it. Nurse Megan was just a huggy zebra.

Matthew's mom explained that Matthew had come up with the idea of bringing the decorations and Coach Keith thanked him.

"What can I do?" asked Michael.

"Coach Justin could use some help with moving tables and hanging Christmas lights," said Nurse Megan.

"That sounds perfect for me," said Michael. "Mom, I will be with Coach Justin if you need me."

Once inside, the family got right to work. Mom headed for the kitchen to get some more baking done. Dad and Coach Keith went to work wrapping presents. Matthew sat at the table and continued to work on the popcorn and cranberry decorations for the tree.

Nurse Megan came over and sat by Matthew. "Mind if I sit here?" she asked. "I have to go over the list of those signed up to make sure that we have enough food and gifts."

"Not at all," said Matthew as he concentrated on his pattern, "How many people are signed up?"

"Quite a few," answered Nurse Megan. "There are a lot of people who need our help."

Matthew glanced over at the list and saw a familiar name. "That's Kevin's name," said Matthew. "He is in my class. What is his name doing on the list?"

"Kevin and his family had a fire at their house not too long ago. He and his family just need a little help until their house is rebuilt."

"Our teacher, Miss Nina, told us about a lemur family that had a fire at their home, but I did not know that it was Kevin's family. He never said anything."

"Maybe he didn't want anyone to know," said Megan.

"Why not?" asked Matthew.

"Maybe he didn't want anyone feeling sorry for him."

"I wouldn't do that," said Matthew. "I would want to help him more because he is my friend."

"That's because you're a very special little monkey," said Megan as she gave Matthew a little hug.

Just then, Matthew's friend Elizabeth and her mom came in to help. "What can I do to help?" asked Elizabeth.

"You can help Matthew string popcorn and cranberries. Then we have to put hooks on the ornaments."

Elizabeth sat down next to Matthew and got started. Her mom went with Nurse Megan to work on the centerpieces for the tables.

"You have done so much by yourself," said Elizabeth. "Everything looks great."

"Thanks," said Matthew as he handed Elizabeth a string and a bowl of popcorn.

"Elizabeth, can I ask you a question?"

"Sure, Matthew, what's up?"

"I know that your dad is in heaven, and I know that you miss him, but do you ever not tell people about that?"

Elizabeth took a breath and answered, "When I first started at the new school and was just meeting new kids in the class, I did not tell them about my dad. Not right away, at least."

"But why?" asked Matthew.

"Mostly because I wanted them to like me, and I did not want anyone to feel sorry for me. I just wanted to be like every-one else."

"But you told me," said Matthew.

"That's because I trusted you, and we became friends right away," said Elizabeth. "Why all the questions?"

"Just wondering," answered Matthew. "We better get going on these decorations. Coach Justin and Michael almost have the tree set up."

For the next hour, everyone worked so hard. Coach Keith thanked them all for their time. The community center had been transformed into a winter wonderland.

"See you all on Thursday," called out Nurse Megan.

On the way home, Dad stopped and picked up a pizza for dinner. At home, Madeline was playing ABC blocks with her babysitter. She clapped when she saw everyone and said, "Mmm, pizza."

Matthew and his family ate their pizza and shared stories about their afternoon at the community center. Matthew told his family about Kevin.

"His family are the ones who had the fire. They are the family we collected all the stuff for in Miss Nina's class," said Matthew. "But Kevin didn't say anything."

"Maybe he wanted his privacy, or maybe he didn't want anyone to feel sorry for him," said dad.

"I know. That's what Nurse Megan and Elizabeth told me, but I don't understand why people would feel sorry for them. I would just want to help."

"That's because you are a true friend and treat everyone the same," said Dad.

Mom added, "We need to respect a person's privacy and let them share when they feel comfortable. Now, how about treating ourselves tonight? We all worked hard today. Let's clean up, put on our pajamas, grab our sleeping bags, and watch a movie."

"Yahoo!" shouted everyone as they all scattered in different directions.

No one was able to stay awake until the end of the movie that night. They were all so tired.

Matthew and his family spent the next day decorating their Christmas tree, wrapping gifts, and cleaning the house. By the time Matthew crawled into bed that night, he was tired, but his mind was spinning. He was thinking about Christmas morning, about the gifts that he made at school for his family. Most of all, he was thinking about seeing his friend Kevin.

Matthew woke to the smell of his favorite blueberry and banana waffles. As he rolled over, he remembered it was Christmas morning. He jumped out of bed and ran down to the kitchen.

"Merry Christmas!" shouted Matthew as he entered the kitchen.

"Merry Christmas to you, sleepyhead," said Mom as she gave him a kiss on the top of his head.

"We have been waiting forever for you to wake up," said Michael. "Come on, and let's open presents."

After Matthew and his family had opened all the gifts, they sat down to eat breakfast. Mom and Dad loved their ornament that Matthew had made for them at school, and Mom had hung it on the tree right away. Matthew had gotten the newest racing DVD. Michael received a baseball hat and jersey from his favorite team that he had been begging for, for a long time, and Madeline got a new baby doll and was carrying it around everywhere.

"We better finish up so that we can get down to the community center," said Dad.

The family finished up and headed for the center. Once there, they greeted everyone, wishing them a Merry Christmas and, of course, getting a hug from Nurse Megan.

The doors opened, and the community center came alive. Matthew was standing next to Coach Keith when he saw Kevin and his family come through the door and head toward a table.

"Penny for your thoughts," said Coach Keith to Matthew.

"What?" asked Matthew.

"It's an expression. You seem to be thinking about something important."

"I see my friend from school, and I am not sure what to say to him," said Matthew.

"How about starting with, 'Merry Christmas'?" asked Coach Keith.

"Good idea," said Matthew as he slowly walked over to where Kevin and his family were seated.

"Merry Christmas, Kevin," said Matthew.

Kevin turned around and saw Matthew. "Um, Merry Christmas to you too, Matthew," said Kevin. Kevin then introduced Matthew to his family.

"*Dinner is ready!*" shouted Coach Justin. "*Come and get it!*"

"I've got to go and help," said Matthew. "Is it okay if I come back and talk?"

"Sure," said Kevin.

The meal was a success. Coaches Keith and Justin handed out gifts to the children. Music was playing. There was a lot of love present at the community center that day.

When things slowed down, Matthew stopped by to see Kevin.

"Hey, Matthew, look! I got the Coconut Pickup game!" said Kevin.

"I love Coconut Pickup!" exclaimed Matthew. "Want to play a game?"

"Sure," said Kevin.

Matthew and Kevin played two games before Matthew got up the courage to ask Kevin the question that had been on his mind for almost three days.

"Kevin, why didn't you say anything at school about the fire being at your house?" asked Matthew.

"I didn't want anyone to feel sorry for me. I just wanted to be your friend," said Kevin. "And I kind of couldn't believe that it really happened."

"I can understand that," said Matthew. "But, Kevin, I will always be your friend. Friends don't care about what you have. They care about you."

"I know that now," said Kevin. "Thanks, Matthew. Now, want me to beat you at another game of Coconut Pickup?"

"Good luck with that," said Matthew as he rolled the coconuts.

That Christmas, Matthew learned about value. Not the value of a thing, but the value of a friendship, and the value of family.

It was the best Christmas ever.